Dinner with the
Cannibal Sisters

Dinner with the
Cannibal Sisters

Douglas Clegg

CEMETERY DANCE PUBLICATIONS

Baltimore
❖ 2014 ❖

Cemetery Dance Publications
132-B Industry Lane, Unit #7
Forest Hill, MD 21050
http://www.cemeterydance.com

The characters and events in this book are fictitious.
Any similarity to real persons, living or dead,
is coincidental and not intended by the author.

First Limited Edition Printing

ISBN-13: 978-1-58767-407-5

Cover & Interior Artwork © 2014 by Caniglia
Cover Design by Desert Isle Design
Interior Design by Kate Freeman Design

For Daniel Waters,

With thanks also to the spectators in the trees, to Caniglia, Richard Chizmar and everyone at Cemetery Dance, Raul, Simon, Melisse, Matt, Kathe, Ann, Norman, and Lizzie Borden.

IN THE FALL OF 1910, SEVERAL MONTHS after Halley's Comet blazed a corner of the sky, I took the train north to meet the famed Windrow sisters. I was not quite twenty, ambitious, with a newborn belief in my brilliant future.

I changed trains three times after New Haven. I ran between tracks, soaked with sweat and held hostage by a cheap wool suit. My route diverted, with more crossings to catch and new trains to chase after.

I didn't think I'd make it to Bog House by nightfall.

At Hartford, my compartment emptied.

As the train jolted to life, a middle-aged gentleman took the seat across. He jotted notes in a furious manner within a small brown leather notebook. A slight nod of greeting, then back to his writing. He wore a farmer's straw hat, which did a poor job of hiding his clean-shaven scalp. A blue kerchief substituted for a tie at his collar.

I looked out the window to the passing countryside. The brick and gray city gave way to flat open land between scattered woods, interrupted by bungalows and blighted Victorians.

"Warm," he said. "For October."

"Too warm."

"Quite a storm last night."

I glanced over. He kept his eyes downcast as he scribbled notes. He'd dropped his hat onto his lap. I couldn't help but notice the smooth contours of his head.

"Hear about the Upson crossing?"

"Don't tell me the bridge is out," I said.

"All right, I won't."

"Another transfer," I groaned, mentioning the village near my ultimate destination.

"Heading to the harvest festival?" He tapped his pencil at the edge of his teeth, watching me. "No wait. Don't tell me. The tie, ragged collar, uncut hair, hat too large for head, packysack. You work for the papers."

"Bullseye." I felt ordained by his guess.

"I've seen the uniform before."

Unable to contain myself, I bragged about my assignment.

His eyes widened slightly.

"I know the area," he said. "I go up there. At times."

He named the excellent dairy—close to the village—famous for its ice cream. The river nearby. The fall foliage. A few family names.

And then, the Windrow place.

His left eye twitched. Out the window, down to his notebook, then back to me. "Hard to believe they'd invite a reporter up."

"I heard from Holbein himself." I told him. "The Moravian."

The gentleman squinted.

"The servant," he said. "He's Dutch."

"Dutch. Moravian. Prussian. Who knows?"

He made a low grunting noise. "An invitation from Holbein."

"From the sisters, too."

"The notorious Lucy and Sally."

"Ever see them?" I asked.

He cocked his head to the side, an inquisitive bird sizing me up. "Years ago. In Boston."

"Their tour?" I asked. "What was it like?"

"Humiliating."

Silence seeped into the space between us, interrupted by the grind and gruff of train. I thought about those girls, the lecture circuit, and the desperate uncle who showed up to claim guardianship—and line his pocket with his nieces' notoriety.

"Well, even so," I said, perking up. "I'm there to spend a few days. Interview them. The twentieth anniversary and all."

"This time of year, a lot of reporters show up at that house, hoping to get a peek."

He paused. "None of them get invitations, though. You're special."

We didn't talk for a minute or more.

He made a noise at the back of his throat. "You'll make up a story, no doubt."

"No, I won't."

"They all do," he said. "Leave them alone. Those poor girls."

But of course, the Windrows weren't girls—not then.

New Englanders in particular protected such families, enclosing them within a secret garden of silence, away from the eyes of the world.

Lizzie Borden—who frequented the theater—ran a lively salon in Fall River. She contributed to animal charities. Those who lived in her hilltop neighborhood argued against the murdered parents themselves and the incestuous nature of wealthy families.

The aptly named Butcher Boy of Beacon Hill, at fifty, walked the streets of Boston after his imprisonment and even made a run for political office.

Edwin Mortimer of Crannock Bay continued to drop his lobster pots out among Maine's islands, despite the strong possibility that he had tossed his wife and children from the edge of a cliff just six years earlier.

And then the Windrows, "the girls"—in their thirties at the time of my journey—protected by an interfering stranger on a train.

Twenty years earlier, the Windrow story set the nation on fire with tales of wealth and madness, horror and pity. A popular rhyme about the girls appeared in print soon after the discoveries. A frenetic dance called "The Cannibal Rag" became popular in the Dance Halls. Illustrated chapbooks and pulps detailed the exploits at The Bog House of Horrors. The newspapers—every year on the anniversary—mentioned the place and its events, but no one got close enough to speak to the Windrow sisters.

Who's that scraping at the window?
Look! It's pretty Lucy Windrow,
She's grown thinner—
And you're a sinner—
She'll serve you up like Christmas dinner.

And just behind her, here comes Sally
Hunting supper in the alley!
Toss you in the pot,
When it's boiling hot—
She'll gobble you down—or watch you rot.

I was seven when I first heard this rhyme.
Girls skipped rope to it. My father told me
never to repeat it. Every child knew it. Even
years later, children still know it, but few understand its origin.

These things get passed down.

No one really blamed the girls—the entire Windrow household had been strange from the outset.

The father—Dr. Thomas Windrow—studied surgery in Boston, specializing in disorders of the mind.

He practiced a peculiar psychiatry that involved little mallets, slender flat blades and small screws—as well as more radical methods. His milder remedies included a series of home-brewed herbal concoctions seemingly drawn from medieval texts.

Developing a type of surgical incision, he named it for himself—the Windrow Method—which he described as cerebral-therapeutic fistulation.

In preparation for the weekend, I'd skimmed his books and the many scientific articles detailing his innovations. I immersed myself in the trial of 1867, regarding Windrow's anatomical studies of Irish maids.

Windrow held it as scientific fact that there existed a ruinous connection between the female brain and that fertile pathway

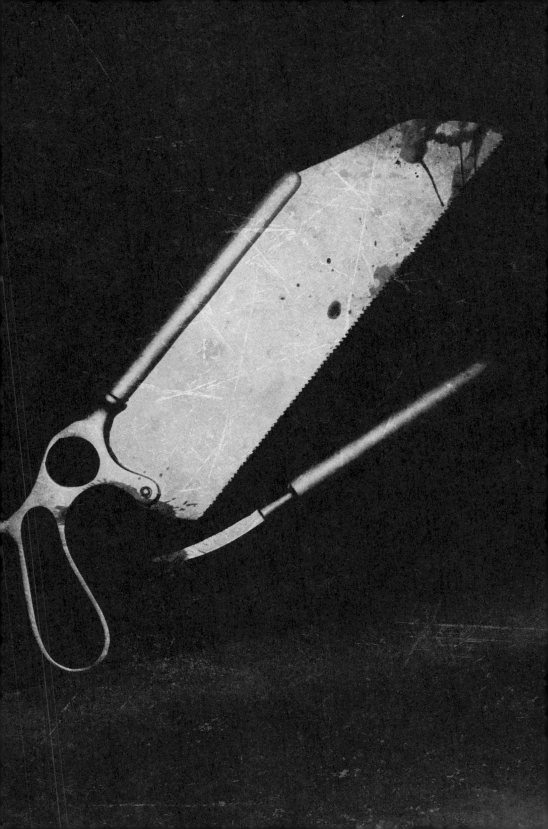

known in those olden days as "the woman's burden."

Acquitted at trial, briefly plagued by rumors of missing women from the poorest of families, Dr. Windrow moved to the countryside of New Hampshire.

He resumed his practice. Well-known by 1870 for the aptly named Body-Repulsion Cure of a Senator's nymphomaniac daughter, his reputation began to repair itself.

At his new home, Dr. Windrow pioneered a trance-based therapy called Somnalocution, which involved communication with disturbed patients in their deepest hours of sleep. This became standard in many asylum hospitals, briefly, until more effective therapies replaced it.

In my own day, traveling magicians practiced the method.

The girls' mother—Judith—had been one of Dr. Windrow's patients.

They met when Dr. Windrow was nearly forty, past his brief flirtation with scandal, well-established, well-regarded, somewhat feared.

Judith Meade was fifteen when she came under Dr. Windrow's care. Daughter of a wealthy charlatan within the spiritualist movement, she suffered from a noisy insomnia, frequent outbursts, and the belief that the spirit world chattered incessantly around her.

She tried to stab her father twice with a kitchen knife before the age of twelve.

Her path to a cure became the subject of Dr. Windrow's fourth book, *The Essential Damage of the Female Mind*.

Thomas and Judith married when she was seventeen—and no longer heard voices. The girls came next, then two little boys, Henry and Jonathan.

Their household consisted of another former patient—Holbein—some farmhands, and Aunt Sapphronia. It was believed that the girls' mother and the aunt regularly held séances at the house.

Aunt Sapphronia became known to locals as the Bog House Witch.

Anyone familiar with the lurid chapbooks would never forget the spinster aunt who occupied the room at the top of the attic stair.

That famous room, as it turned out.

In those days, few people trusted physicians—particularly doctors of the mind. Dr. Windrow always had his critics. Denounced from pulpits, he was barred from prestigious medical clubs and academic gatherings, as well.

Yet few could argue with his success rate.

An attempt had been made in the late 1880s—by Judith's relatives—to free mother and children from what these uncles and aunts termed "the obsessive and destructive nature of the abnormal situation of this abominable home laboratory."

This ended when Judith herself sent word to the local authorities to remove—by force—her disruptive relations for "trespassing, robbery, and corruption of children."

Still others—particularly the loved ones of those cured by Windrow's radical methods—praised the family. Wealthy patrons lavished gifts of money upon Dr. Windrow's practice. They wrote letters to newspapers supporting his methods, even after the initial, grisly discoveries.

By all accounts, Bog House—prior to the events of the fateful October day in 1890—had become a therapeutic farm with dairy and pastures for a smattering of sheep, goats and cows. Patients resided in dormitories within the converted barn and stables—a place known as Bright Colony.

The mentally ill arrived from brutal asylums for Dr. Windrow's unusual cures. These patients labored beneath the hot summer sun, ate wild berries and root vegetables, milled local grains, tasted creamery butter, and chewed the leaves of oddly named herbs.

According to the local wags, patients took moon-baths—naked—on straw mats after midnight in the open air, spied upon by delinquent sons of the village.

In winter, activities included standing in the icy bog for a quarter-hour at a time, dervish-style spinning, snow-sitting, and the use of bound birch twigs for mutual and presumably healthful flagellation after a long sweat-bath.

Residents of neighboring farms didn't love catching sight of wild-haired hysterics wandering open fields at mid-day. Now and then, a nymphomaniac or homosexual would escape to the village—always a danger to the well-being of a populace.

Nor did any of the locals appreciate the rumors of Bog House life. Free love; unbridled nakedness; spirit trances; libertinism; animalistic games; field dancing; incantatory chanting; wild children; agonized screeches; unconventional therapies; escaped patients.

When the events of that fateful October weekend came to pass, those who knew the Windrow situation were not surprised.

Something about the Windrow girls struck a chord of deep sympathy among those who followed the father's work.

The early photos of the cellar and the then-legendary room up the attic stair. The father's medical career—the worst of which came to light during the days after. The isolation of the house out along bog and woods. Farmhands who vanished soon after delivering the girls to the authorities. The pitiful mad-folk running through the woods. The abattoir with its strange cargo. Ungodly surgical instruments. Vials of nightshade, mandrake root and snake venom. The broken Ouija. Rubble of surgery in the cellar. Black goat in the living room. Photographs of men and women in "unmentionable positions."

Eyewitnesses to these mysteries and discoveries spoke of the misfortune of any child born to such a life.

And then there were the maps.

Over the years, some squalid magazine or scandal sheet would publish one of these maps, later to be exposed as a forgery.

The maps themselves became part of the legend.

Up to this moment, traveling to Bog House, I worked as a printer's assistant in a news office.

I wanted to write feature stories, to be at the match, covering the tragedy, digging in the history of things, exposing political corruption, interviewing great men of the day, taking the pulse of my city and nation.

Instead, I set type and watched my life pass by.

Between wars and news of border skirmishes, scandal and sensationalism sold papers. In those days, people liked such tales. Murders, robberies, lurid confessions of ruinous seduction, kidnappings, the fall of the wealthy, the secrets and loves of immoral theater people—even the legends of the Old West—all held a strong draw for those wishing to skip the financial section.

But to truly sell-out a paper, there existed nothing quite so potent as the direct confession of a killer, particularly one whose depravity stood the test of time.

When the Lonely-Hearts Killer, Joshua Leland of Fairpark, Long Island, passed ribbon-bound, perfumed correspondence to Alec Marsh at a family-owned pawnshop in Brooklyn, who could guess it would transform Marsh's world? Alec Marsh worked part-time at the shop, but also wrote brief column items for the *Press-Herald*.

Alec Marsh befriended Leland, taking him for drinks, not so accidentally running into him along the shoreline village. Confiding in Leland about his own love troubles, Marsh expressed a righteous fury about the female's power over the male in affairs of the heart.

The trick worked. Joshua Leland soon spoke openly to Marsh about the trophies he'd buried along the dunes.

The evidence gathered, a confession made—in print—and Leland practically hanged himself, nearly fourteen years after the murders.

From this series of articles, Alec Marsh became one of the most famous newspapermen in the country. Magazine serials followed, then a book deal, a touring lecture, and the kind of fame most reporters would sell their grandmothers for. He seemed extraordinarily well off, married a popular actress of the moment, and lived in the best part of the city.

I went to hear him speak at the Astor Library. I was surprised to see that he was such a young man. His entire career, I thought, turning upon a chance conversation with an odd little man wearing spectacles and a straw boater wanting a loan in exchange for "valuable love letters from much-sought-after women."

Alec Marsh played his cards right and won the game.

I became convinced that the Windrow confession would be my prize.

Every October—for years—distinguished journalists and reporters tramped through the New Hampshire woods to get some word from Lucy or Sally Windrow, only to return with vague rumblings of secondhand information.

By the luck of blood—that is to say, my maternal great-grandmother's blood—I discovered that the Windrows were distant cousins by marriage. When I confronted my mother with this genealogy, she cringed and shaded her eyes from the afternoon glare. "Maybe some Windrows, but not those Windrows."

Still, it was enough for me to go to the editor's office and convince him of my worthiness.

I reminded him that this particular autumn marked the twentieth anniversary of the event at Bog House. I thumbed through program booklets of recent revivals of scandalous biographies and murder stories on the stage, with frequent reference to the Windrows.

I mentioned the upcoming novel called *The Cannibal Sisters* that a bestselling writer of that hour would publish to coincide with the anniversary, and how the *Times*, *Post* and *Evening Star* tried to snag an interview with the girls but could not pull it off.

I delivered a glancing blow: Dr. Crippen, not yet on trial in London, an American by birth—how many thousands of newspapers had sold-out overnight with news of the grisly discovery in his cellar, his strange paramour called *Le Neve* disguised as a boy on shipboard, and the transatlantic chase on the White Star Line by the intrepid Inspector Dew.

"Long after Crippen's old news," I told my boss, dimming the desk lamp, reaching over to draw the shades against afternoon glare, speaking with as much drama as I could muster, "the Windrow sisters will still be the great nightmare that keeps readers buying newspapers. We're all hungry for details of these pretty ogresses and their larder—from your paper and no one else's."

I held my hands up, setting invisible scenes in the air above my editor's desk. Resonance burst in my voice. I rehearsed these lines for three days. I knew my boss and his way of thinking. I tailored everything to him.

"But they're more than some…some Penny Dreadful kind of thing. Ask anyone who remembers. The photos of these girls, lovely as roses, in the bloom of maidenhood," I said. "A famous doctor, strange medical practices, a pastoral asylum—a rampage! We know the local authorities tried to pin it on the patients, on the atmosphere, on those never caught. The legal maneuvering they had—the finest lawyers—the best money could buy. The girls—beloved in that region—and pitied. Pitied! No one wanted to believe two young ladies could ever commit such acts of savagery. But is that the true story? No one knows. No one. No one's gotten close enough to find out. No reporter has gotten a first-hand interview from them."

I paused, caught my breath, watching my editor's face.

I imagined victory in the slight twitch of smile that began at the left corner of his mouth.

I leaned over his desk, looking him directly in the eye. "Don't forget Joshua Leland. Don't forget Crippen. The Windrow sisters are bigger fish. They've got the girlhood angle, the medical angle, the insulating wealth. They've been silent for twenty years. But this will end. They'll tell the tale in their own words of the night that shocked the world."

And then, I closed my case: "And they'll only speak to me—their cousin."

This is a long way toward confessing that I lied repeatedly and tied my somewhat distant connection ever closer to the sisters. I omitted the fact that I'd written to Bog House several times over the past year, without response.

I stabbed deep wounds into the heaving breast of truth, desperate for this opportunity to make my future.

And there I was—train crossings and transfers behind me, a night spent at a shabby inn halfway to nowhere, a day late, in that village a good distance from the Windrow place.

By noon, I persuaded a local to give me a ride. I sat at the back of a horse-drawn wagon headed down a dirt highway that would lead to somber woods, toward Bog House.

The sun crossed the sky. The wagon lurched along the road, leaving me at the start of a well-worn path.

I stepped within an aisle of poplars to the beginning of Windrow land.

I expected fences and warning signs, but found none. I passed evidence of a campfire from some previous squatter—another reporter, perhaps—by a pond that smelled of sulfur. Shoeprints all around had dried in mud, fossil evidence of those who had come before. A small doe darted between pine and shafts of sunlight.

The path meandered through woods, abandoning me to open field.

By the time the house came into view it was not yet dark, but slouching in that direction.

I felt hungry and exhausted. Nearly there, I thought. Nearly there.

Just ahead: a cloud of smoke.

I came upon a man burning bramble and dried grass.

"Get out," he said, back toward me.

By his accent, I assumed this was the Moravian. Or Dutchman.

He turned about. Foul language burst from his lips—at least, I assumed it was foul, though spoken in some foreign tongue.

In ragged English, he said, "You get out! Now! You stay after dark, you never leave. Understand?"

I stood my ground.

He reached for a shovel, hefting it in one hand. He pushed it right into the fire. Bringing up a flaming branch, he swung the shovel around so that the burning wood nearly touched my face.

"I'm their cousin," I said.

He raised the flaming shovel and sliced the air between us.

"I'm their cousin!" I shouted.

He thrust the shovel into the dirt. The fiery moment passed. He pointed at me, his finger grazing the buttons of my shirt. More foreign words came out of him.

He stomped off toward the house, turning around several yards ahead to fix me with the evil eye.

Away from the smoldering mess, I sat down in full view of Bog House and opened my canvas sack. Pushing aside my rolled-up coat and a change of clothes, I brought out my notebook and pencil. I scribbled about

the journey, the village and region, my first impressions, and Holbein's greeting.

I wrote down the names Lucy and Sally with question marks, and jotted brief notes for further inquiry.

I greedily devoured the fried egg sandwich I'd bought in the village that morning, and drank the last of my water flask.

I wondered if Holbein might return and stab the shovel's edge into my throat—all of this ending with me being cooked up on a platter in time for dinner.

It was less than an hour until the sun would go down, and a long way back to the main road.

As I watched the house, twilight deepened. Locusts and night birds interrupted purple silence. Bats peppered the sky along the fringe of trees.

Could anyone call this Bog House? An upright farmhouse, gray from time and neglect, smaller than one would expect—given the Windrow money—and entirely ordinary.

I saw no barn nearby—no Bright Colony—no abattoir. No side buildings, no stables, nothing to indicate an actual farm.

Lights came up in the front windows. A slender vein of smoke rose from the chimney.

A woman stepped out on the rounded porch. She lit the lamps along its rail. She gazed across the field, her hands beside her mouth as she called out the name "Catherine" a few times.

Not a moment after her last call, a blur of movement raced from the western woods toward the house. I guessed it was a large dog of some unusual breed, but retained the impression that the animal was not quite dog at all.

After the creature bounded up the steps, its mistress leaned over the rail and looked directly at me—or so I felt—and then turned toward the screen door.

She spoke to someone lurking just inside the house.

When she came down the front steps, she walked her pet by a long leash, and—in her other hand—carried a lantern.

I stood up as mistress and animal came within a few feet of me.

This was no dog on a leash: the Windrow sister walked a cheetah, sleek and elegant as any creature I'd ever seen.

The Windrow woman tugged at the lead, guiding the cat back to her side.

She crouched, setting the lantern just between us. She lifted its brass lid. The flame inside leaped a little, illuminating her as if she were an actress standing before the footlights.

Was this Lucy or Sally? Her face seemed familiar—the bridge of her nose, her eyes—my recollection of the photographs from old books, perhaps. Barefoot, she wore a long silky black dress printed with gold geometric designs that caught the light. It seemed very modern, very arty and rich bohemian, born from Manhattan or perhaps even Paris, not so much New Hampshire farm.

Her hair, pulled back from her face, flew wild and curly about her ears and forehead. She had what my mother would've called a companionable handsomeness, not quite beauty or prettiness, but something even more compelling: a feeling of being at home in her presence.

"Holly says you're our cousin." She tilted her chin up. She touched my ear and then pressed lightly on my nose.

She stepped back. "You're one of Auntie Rags' brood?"

"I'm afraid not."

"Oh," she lightly slapped her forehead, "Auntie Mary, I mean. Your father would be Harold."

When she mentioned my parents' names, I opened my mouth slightly.

"Yes."

"You look like our grandmother, too," she continued. "Meade-side, of course. That old lady had nine children, mostly girls. Our mothers weren't close in age. I think there's a fifteen-year gap. Mama always called her 'little ragamuffin' when we were young, so we knew her as Auntie Rags, mostly. She probably despised that nickname. I don't blame her, but we meant it with love." Then, turning to the cheetah, "Catherine. Sit. Sit. Come on, sit."

The cheetah lay down in the grass, rolling on its side. It began licking its paws. The Windrow woman dropped the leash in the dirt.

"Is that safe?" I asked.

"What—Catherine? She's not as tough as she looks."

I glanced between Windrow and wildcat. I didn't know whom to trust less.

"Last time I saw your mother was…" She counted her fingers. "Well, she was youngish. Before you were born, I know that much! Rags loved games—she was always savage at croquet. A bit on the cheaty side. Nobody minded, not really. How *is* your mother?"

"Still savage at croquet. Doing well."

"Good. Sorry we had a falling out. I hate loose ends."

The sun had not quite vanished beyond the grasp of trees. "It's suddenly so murky—this time of night. And cold, too, after such a hot, hot, hot day. It means winter's got its back up." She reached up and stole my hat, spinning it in her hand. "A gentleman takes his hat off in the presence of a lady."

"Sorry," I said.

"Don't be—I'm teasing. We don't exactly follow rules here."

She blinked as she looked at me. In the deepening shadows, I almost felt a spark leap between us.

She crouched down by the lantern box, closing its lid.

Rising, she brought the light, waving it near my face. "Let me get a good look, just to be sure."

She swung it left to right. No woman had ever studied my features before. "You inherited the Meade look. My sister and I—well, we ended up with a bit more Windrow in us."

"I didn't know there was a Meade look," I said.

"Honestly, you look more like Rags by the second."

"I hope that's a compliment."

"I'd never say it otherwise," she said. "Why, the best-looking men I've met look almost exactly like pretty women."

Passing the lantern, she pulled my hat snugly down over her frothy hair. "Do you mind? I love a good headdress."

"It looks better on you than on me."

"Think so? Wait—is it a gift?"

I laughed. "I don't know."

"You can't come in the house without giving a gift."

"All right," I said. "It's for you. A gift."

"Thank you. How thoughtful—I love it!" She turned to go back to the house, snapping her fingers at the cheetah. The cat slinked along beside her, dragging its lead.

Miss Windrow spun around to face me, walking backward. "You'll stay for dinner? Holly's been working his magic in the kitchen, but it puts him in a bad mood. You'll love him, anyway. He's one of those people you can't help but love, even at his worst. And believe me, I've seen him on his stormy days. He can be very, very wicked."

"If Holly is Holbein, then I think we've met. Over there." I pointed to the area where Holbein had raised the flaming shovel at me. "At his worst, I guess."

She pretended not to know what I was talking about. "He's been inside mostly. Stirring pots. Taming wild sauces. Chopping fennel and dill. We'd starve if he weren't so good at it. It runs in his family. You'll definitely stay?"

"Of course." I reached forward, grabbing her forearm to steady her. "You know, if you keep walking backward like that, you're liable to fall."

"But you'll catch me," she said, wriggling free from my grasp. She turned forward and then stopped, waiting for me. "I just realized something. Your name. I don't know it."

I told her, and she said it back to me in a whisper. "But I don't know yours, Miss Windrow."

"Everybody knows *my* name." Her mood changed when she glanced over my shoulder. "You'd think they'd just go home by now."

"Who?"

"*Them*."

I looked back at the darkening wood. I thought of the ashes of the campfire. The impressions in dried mud.

"Out there. In the trees. All over. Cowards." She clenched her fists, raising them to the sky. "Cowards! Come out!"

Her voice echoed across the meadow.

Quieting, she whispered, "Boils my blood. I'm told it's just the way things are. I need to get used to it, she keeps telling me. But I can't."

She ran down the path as if she were going to charge these unseen trespassers. She cupped her hands to the side of her mouth. "You'd think you'd have better things to do! One night I'll set these woods on fire and cook you all up!"

The cheetah trotted over to her.

I scanned the horizon, seeing nothing other than field and trees. Then, in a heavily wooded area, I thought I saw movement. Or had I imagined it?

I walked through the tall grass to stand beside her.

"It's all right," I said, with nothing else for comfort. "I think they're gone."

As I reached her, she turned toward me, her face in darkness. An urge rose up in me—a child-like impulse to hold her the way one might cup a small bird, its wing broken, in one's hands.

"Imagine," she whispered. "Spending your life spying like that."

The cheetah growled, sniffing the air.

The unnamed Windrow sister bent down to pet the cat behind its ears. "You need to eat them all up, Catherine." Then, in a kind of baby talk, "Catherine the Great is feeling sad today. She's been on the hunt and hasn't even come home with a wabbit. Not a single wabbit."

She led me back to the house, my hat on her head.

I wagged the lantern, following.

At the front step, she touched my arm. "I have to warn you—Lucy doesn't love unannounced visitors. Tread softly around her. I'm going to fib a bit. Say that I invited you. She's just afraid, that's all. We've got to be careful."

So this was Sally, I thought. The younger of the two. The one who saved the ears, hiding them in the china cupboard so that she could have them all to herself.

This—my cousin—was the cannibal girl who growled like a cheetah herself when she'd been found.

We moved past the screen door, through the parlor with its upright piano and cushioned chairs, into the wide, overstuffed living room.

The cheetah trailed its mistress. I kept a few paces behind the cat. Sally breathlessly named little framed paintings and mezzotints on the walls, guiding me to favorite books on shelves, apologizing for the irregular stacks of *The Delineator* and *Ladies' Home Journal* strewn around high-backed chairs.

Strangely, she turned down lamps as she led me through the maze.

I squinted to make out items in the dusky room: small figurines of children and birds in rows along window sills, the floor painted with a series of fiery swirls, an empty bird-cage on a metal stand, shadows of corner chairs, a tall bronze of the god Mercury be-side an antique globe.

"Notice anything?" Sally asked, as she turned down yet another lamp.

"Well, everything," I said. "There's so much here."

"You're looking down too much," she said, but I didn't understand her at the time, nor did I question her judgment in darken-ing the room.

Finally, nearing the center, she turned up a table lamp just enough to dispel shadows.

Beside the lamp lay a Ouija board so battered and ancient that I wondered if it belonged to the notorious Aunt Sapphronia.

"We pass the time here on quiet nights, playing games until one of us grows tired of losing—or we get all goopy and silly. Sometimes I just sit here and look up at the stars."

A feeble fire spat and sputtered in the small fireplace, distracting me from her face. A large blue dish full of colored marbles rested near the hearth. Playing cards were stacked unevenly beside a checkered *Halma* board scattered with black and white pawns. One long table held a near-complete jigsaw puzzle of children frolicking behind the Pied Piper of Hamelin.

Odors mingled—the sauces and steam and onion sting from the kitchen; the smell of mothballs and cedar from a doorless wardrobe piled high with furs; smoky pine at the fireplace; a sweetness of late-blooming flowers, puffballs of yellow, red, green and white, stuffed in crystal bowls on a table by a wide window.

"All right, it's a mess," Sally said. "I keep promising to clean it all up tomorrow—and tomorrow never quite shows up. We used to have a girl from the village to keep it tidy. She stopped showing up, too. I think Holly frightened her."

She called for the servant.

After a moment, Holly stepped in from the hall, turning up lights. His face shone with sweat. He wore a white apron with small blue flowers embroidered on it. He pushed his straw-blond hair behind his ears—one of which held a ruby, pierced at the lobe. He waved a large wooden spoon around as if conducting a silent orchestra.

Sally introduced us; we nodded to each other.

"I think you'll like the feast tonight," he said, his accent less heavy than when he'd threatened me. "Sorry about the shovel. Perhaps you understand?"

I nodded. "Of course."

"It's to keep out riff-raff," he said. "If I'd known you were family, I wouldn't have been so…so ferocious. You must forgive me. So many horrible people come out of the woods these days."

We settled the Moravian-Dutch question: his mother was Austrian, his father, Dutch, but yes, he told me, there was some Moravian and even Russian. "Like my recipes—a little of this, a pinch of that," he winked.

Sally pointed to the cheetah. "Holly, take Catherine to her cage. Only one chop for tonight. She's slowing down in her old age." Sally admonished her pet, "No wabbits, no cookies."

Holly took the leash and exchanged a few whispers with Sally before heading back to the kitchen.

"She sleeps in a cage some nights," Sally said. "I hate doing it to her, but awhile back she tore the kitchen up. I shouldn't feel guilty—she gets the whole day to run in the woods. Do you have pets?"

"A dog," I said, feeling inadequate. "Not really mine. It's my father's."

"We had a dog, years ago," she said. "An absolute failure at chasing off those kinds of people, you know, the kind that lurk in the woods and then come out to gawk. Catherine growls them away—usually—but not tonight, obviously. I don't know how anyone deals with this kind of thing, do you? How do you deal with it? Those sorts of people?"

As she drifted off in stories of strangers camping out on the front porch every October like clockwork, it dawned on me that she had no idea that people might be showing up because of what happened in the fall of 1890. She assumed everyone had strangers coming by, trying to annoy, to get into the house, to take souvenirs.

Sally Windrow and her sister had never been away from this house, with the exception of two weeks of the lecture tour, when the world seemed to record their every move.

"This is my new love," Sally cooed as she led me over to the Victrola.

She shimmied a dark record from its brown paper sleeve. "It's smart, don't you think?"

She put the record on the turntable, winding the crank. A chorus began singing the recent hit, "School Days," through a crackling skip of the needle.

Sally turned and clapped her hands. "I could just listen to record after record. Want to pick one?" She gestured toward a stack of recordings piled on the floor. "We try to get the latest, but we're not always up on what the younger set listen to."

We went through the records. I picked out some favorites, almost forgetting my reason for being at Bog House.

When we put another recording on, the explosive blast of a car horn startled us.

Someone drove up to the house.

"That car," Sally said. "I hate automobiles. Hate them. They have to be the smelliest, most disgusting machines in the world. Cost a fortune, the coupe, but Mama used to call her Lucy-Gotta-Get-It. If it's new, if it's fancy, Lucy wants it. She loves her cars—until she crashes them."

I followed Sally down a many-doored hallway, through the kitchen with its jungle smells of spice and meat with Holly—mad alchemist—running between oven and stove and bowls and elixirs. We went past Catherine the Great in her enormous and well-appointed cage, out the back door, down creaky steps.

An automobile growled along the bumpy road to the house, swerving onto the grass, turning this way and that before coming to a stop just a few yards from where we stood.

"I should've warned you," she said. "She's here with an old friend of ours. He stayed over last night. After what seems like a century, Lucy's finally won him over to her dark nature. I'm a bit more prickly with my affections.

I tend to tear men up, as Catherine the Great might do."

She smiled, offering a little laugh.

The shadow of a woman leapt out from behind the wheel of a Waverley coupe. Lucy Windrow bounded around the front of the car into the light, turning her head first to me, then toward her sister.

Moving between back porch lamp and headlights, Lucy was clothed in the opulent garb of a city woman—long skirt, wide of hip, narrow of ankle, and the Boulevardier with its ostrich feather, drawn back to show her forehead.

She took her hat off. Shaking her hair out, she looked at her sister but pointed in my direction.

Sally drew her aside, out of the light. They carried on a lively conversation of whispers.

A noise distracted me—the other Windrow guest emerged from the car, slamming the door. He stepped out from the shadows and strode up to me.

I recognized him as my inquisitor from the train: the shaven head, the blue kerchief, the farmer's hat.

"Didn't think I'd see you again," I said, once I'd recovered from the surprise.

"But I suspected I'd run into you." He laughed. "I ride back and forth three times a week. If you hadn't been in such a hurry last night, we'd have offered you a lift."

"Quite a coincidence, being here," I said, meaning in fact, that it seemed no coincidence at all.

"Throw a rock on that train—in early October—and three out of five times, you hit somebody from your line of work. Still, none of them managed to get as far as the house. Good going."

"Sally believes they're all over the woods— up in the trees, practically."

"She's probably right." He reached for my hand. No last name, he was just Stefan, an artist and revolutionary and world-appreciationist, but not in that order. "She know why you're here?"

"Yes," I said.

"Well, I suppose that's a good thing, honesty." He came around and put an arm over my shoulder. "Look. I can drive you to the village, later. There's a nice little inn off Market Street—lumpy bed, soggy breakfast, old haggish thing running the place—even electric lights. You'll love it."

"I'm staying the night," I said. "Here."

"I'd advise leaving." He gave my shoulder a slight squeeze. "This is a dangerous situation. Cannibals, boy, cannibals."

Holly clattered around the stove and cupboards as we passed through the hot kitchen. Lucy needed a good lie-down after an entire day spent driving. She wouldn't look my way at all. Sally feigned a headache to get out of socializing. It was obvious they were angry with each other.

"It's your charm," Stefan said.

He and I went out to the front porch. A light mist drifted in off the bog. Stefan stood next to me, back against the rail. He lit up a pipe.

After a minute, I said, "So what kind of revolutionary are you? Anarchist? Or just someone who eats vegetables?"

"A pacifist," he said. "A naturist. Someone who believes in the nature of things, those things not considered. I used to do what you do."

"You wrote for the papers?"

"War got me into it. Then, the lure of travel. The Philippines, China, Mexico, and every place in between. I was young. I believed in what we all believed. But that stopped one day."

When he'd finished his smoke, Stefan guided me back through the house. I glanced in the rooms, each piled up with boxes and furniture. He walked ahead of me into one of the rooms off the hall.

"This was my first commission here. Nearly ten years ago."

I stood beside him as he turned up the lamp.

Two floor-to-ceiling portraits of the girls leaned against the wall. Other paintings of animals—including Catherine the Great—and of the farm itself were propped all around. But I kept returning to those portraits of the Windrow sisters.

"They were in their twenties. A perfect moment, but they were very different then," he said. "They seem younger now."

Lucy—her hair a burning red—wore an oriental silk dressing gown, clasped a thin brown cigarette in one hand, and a paper fan in the other. A faint line of smoke rose from her nostrils.

"She's practically breathing fire," he said. "Magnificent. She let nothing hold her back."

"The light," I said, as I stepped up to the painting and traced a line in the air from the smoke to the fan.

"I lit her from above, below, behind." He came forward, tracing parallel lines in the shadows at Lucy's neck. "You see how it's done? Very stagey—like limelight. I bathed the whole area in light—with paint—and then darkened it gradually for the subject to come through from the light itself."

In the next portrait, Sally stood in a stiff dress that faded into a dark background. Her hair, pulled back in a braid. Her eyes seemed smudged with coal dust. The artist captured her in a sad month.

"With that one, she wanted to disappear. I turned down the light and began with darkness. I call it decandescence."

"What's that mean?"

"It's when you've got to hunt for the light," he said. He waved his hand as if it were a fish swimming upward along Sally's arms. "I darkened nearly everything—but this."

He brought my attention to the gold locket tied with a thin ribbon at Sally's throat. "There's the light. The portrait wouldn't have worked without that locket. With decandescence, the light is always in the last place you'd think to look."

He drew his watch out, checking it.

"Want a drink?"

He led me into the dining room, picked out a crystal bottle and poured burnt amber liquid into two bowl-like glasses.

"Cognac," he said. "You don't drink it, you breathe it."

Within a quarter hour, I'd inhaled a second glass and opened up too much. I began to trust him. We talked of the news business, of painters and sculptors. I managed to bluff my way through the conversation. We talked of everything except Sally and Lucy.

He poured out his past—the assignments, then the features he'd done as he'd grown less interested in the world and more interested, he said, "in smaller things."

"Like?" I asked.

"Those without powerful voices."

"I want the career you had. And you didn't even want it."

He patted me on the back. "Your life's just beginning. I'm in my forties. Time changes. You see things from a distance. What made sense at your age makes less sense. What makes you get up in the morning changes, too."

"And Lucy?"

"What about her?"

"She makes you get up in the morning?"

"We're friends. And I paint a lot when I'm here. I've painted a half-dozen *trompe l'œils* and other little touches around the place, too."

"In the living room. The floor," I said, remembering the swirls beneath my feet.

"You'll find other things like that, if you look up, down and all around," he said. "But you want all that legend of Bog House nonsense that happened before. Still sells papers, doesn't it?"

I nodded. "So you didn't arrive until…"

"1900. On the dot. I'd seen them before. But not here."

"Holbein *was* here for the 1890 event, though," I said.

"You mean Holly? Well, he was—and he wasn't."

I waited for him to explain.

"How old do you think he is?"

A moment's hesitation as I remembered lines on Holly's face, the creases by his eyes. "I don't know. Mid-forties?"

"Try thirty." He took a sip of cognac. "They locked him up for almost a year. A little boy. It aged him. He's got no memory of that year at all."

"All the reports I read made him out to be older…"

"That would be the father. The famous suicide in the abattoir. Holly's mother died six years ago, the family cook right up to her last breath. They were both patients—at one time. Well, half the village used to be residents at Bright Colony."

"Half the village?"

"I exaggerate to make a point," he replied. "Maybe three of them. Or so. Including that madwoman who runs the local inn."

The sharp clang of a bell pierced the air.

"Holly loves ringing the cowbell," Stefan said. "The girls'll be washing up. You'll like the grub. My advice? Don't bring up this stuff over dinner—and watch what you eat. You never know."

I didn't feel truly drunk until I sat down to the table in the dining room.

A mild but unrelenting fear thrummed through my system: had I been drugged? Was Stefan part of some cannibal conspiracy, meeting me first on the train to assess my food value? Was this friendliness a charade to toss me in the pot? Were Stefan's stories of travel and reportage simply the ranting of a former patient of Dr. Windrow's?

The cognacs I'd downed didn't help dispel such thoughts.

Holly laid a Spanish cloth over the long mahogany table.

While setting out the candles in silver holders, he told a story about the region in Spain where his mother bought the tablecloth. His mother first worked with her own mother in some of the famous kitchens of Europe. He learned to cook at her side from his birth onwards, he told us, and nearly became part of a cake's filling at the age of four months when he took a tumble in batter. Lighting each candle, Holly rattled off his early life: he'd made his first soufflé by five, a roast beef by nine, and conjured a four-course dinner for twelve before he turned eleven years old.

As Holly passed behind my chair, he touched my shoulder lightly. "You're here on a special night, my friend."

His further culinary adventures encircled us as he set out the china, gold-leafed, with designs of larks and peacocks perched on the rim of each bowl. Silverware—dull and ancient—clattered as it dropped from Holly's over-large hands.

When Holly vanished back to the kitchen again, I revived the Moravian-Dutch debate. Stefan chuckled at my inability to let that one go. He argued—in a friendly way—that he didn't think an Austrian mother made Holly any less Dutch.

We both went silent when Holly returned, his arms laden with several bottles of red and white wine.

Soon after, bowls and platters whisked in, overflowing with dark berries, bursts of fresh mint, sugar apple medallions, blanched asparagus spears, hibiscus-cranberry jam, slender green and red peppers, breads, sauces and a variety of garnishes.

By this time, Lucy appeared at the doorway in the same dressing gown she'd worn for her portrait. She'd circled her fingers and wrists with a variety of gems and jewels. She sparkled as she walked into the dining room. Her hair, golden, was held in place by a slim diadem as if this were a night out at Delmonico's.

Stefan called her the Queen of the Bog, raising a glass.

Before Sally showed up, we heard her baby-talk to the cheetah in the kitchen, and then, in she swept.

"Holly, this all looks so beautiful—look at the berries! They ripened so late this year. I thought we'd lost them," she said. "And my little peppers! Look at them, cozy babies all snug in bed." She glanced at her sister. "Anyone want music?"

"No," Lucy said.

"Maybe something soft and classical?" Sally went over and gently put her hand on Lucy's shoulder, leaning in, whispering. I caught the phrase, "best behavior."

Stefan—who'd been at the window—sat down beside me, opposite Lucy.

"Everyone looks so handsome," Sally gushed. "This is a special night. I insist on music. Save me a place." She left the room, presumably to crank the Victrola.

"She's like Christmas morning," Stefan said. "You'd think we had the President for a visit."

"Over here," Lucy said, nodding toward him.

After a moment's hesitation, Stefan went to sit beside her.

In a minute, the sound of violins came in from the living room.

"Seems we're playing musical chairs," Sally said when she returned. She glanced at Lucy, and then over to me. "You mind?"

I stood to pull out a chair as she walked around to my side of the table.

"Such a gentleman," Lucy said, unfolding her napkin. To Stefan, "You could learn a thing or two from him." To me, "So how old are you, exactly?"

"Nineteen," I said.

Lucy gave her sister the eye. She reached over and spooned berries onto her side plate. "A bit young."

Leaning over the table, Lucy asked to see my hand. Unsure of her reason, I thrust my arm out and she stood to lean further across the table. I stood, too, awkward as I clutched the table edge with my free hand to keep from falling into the hollandaise.

Lucy held my wrist in her hand. "Not a worker's hands. But look, here's your lifeline. Not bad, not bad. You'll outlive the rest of us."

Stefan chuckled. "Of course he will. He's not even twenty."

"And this," she said as she traced a faint scar left over from my childhood. "This means you'll meet an older woman and fall recklessly in love."

Her eyes narrowed as she scanned between my hand, my face and Sally.

I began to think of her as a python about to unhinge its jaws—but I suppose this was my recall of stories from her younger years, when Lucy allegedly strung up one of her little brothers, at least according to the author of *The Illustrated History of the Bog House Horror*.

I wriggled my hand from her grasp.

"She's in a mood," Sally whispered as I sat down. "Ignore her."

I noticed the locket—the one from the portrait. Sally had it on a slim gold chain around her neck.

"That's pretty," I said, hoping to sound natural. "Your locket."

"Oh," she said, reaching up to touch it. She turned back to the others. She regaled me with stories of Stefan's great work—the paintings he did that hung in the Governor's mansion, the ones of the children down in Rhinebeck and the alms-house in Little Orange.

Holly brought in the first course—a thick broth with hints of herb and meat.

Before I tasted it, I glanced at Stefan who winked at me. Lucy saw the wink and raised an eyebrow. None of this put me at ease. I tasted the soup, and felt a strange tickling in my throat, almost a stinging sensation. I wondered again if I were being drugged or poisoned, but the sensation soon grew into delight.

The room took on a rosy glow from the candles. The cognac settled in at the back of my skull. I felt transported to the kind of glamorous warmth of close family, truly good friends, a place of trust and good times. Infused with the soup's heat, my spirits lifted, no longer weighted by fear or anxiety, almost unclothed with happiness.

"Oh, this is divine," Sally said when Holly returned to check on us. "Holly, what's in this? Is it from the garden?"

"A secret," he said.

"I can taste leek. I know this stuff is celery." Sally inspected a wide spoonful. "With hints of coriander. "

"It's an old recipe," Holly confessed. "My mother would make it a long time ago, on special occasions."

Lucy leaned across the table. "She was cook to the mad Alejandra of Toledo."

"Also, my grandmother was in the kitchen of the Empress of Austria. This is where the recipe comes from I think," Holly said.

"It's delicious," I blurted, unsure of myself.

"Of course it is," Holly said, grinning ear-to-ear. "It's the soup of joy."

"How come we've never had it before?" Sally asked.

Without answering, Holly left the room, shaking his head, mumbling about having forgotten a dish.

Sally leaned in, "He likes you. And he's not fond of many people."

Stefan picked up a bottle of wine and began pouring for Sally and Lucy, passing them back their glasses, spilling some on the cloth.

"Try the red," Stefan said, tipping the bottle in my direction. Before he had another opportunity to stain the tablecloth, I picked up my glass and held it across the table for him. He filled it to near-overflowing. Lucy asked me what it was like living in New York City. I drank, spoke a bit about my little corner of the city, and various new buildings going in and what the theater was like. Glasses clinked and brief toasts competed with each other as we went round and round. "To the last good days of the year," "to the comet," "to dear old Maude, how she loved her drink," "to the horrible Cuban hurricane," "santé," "proost," and "cin-cin."

By my third glass of red, the next course landed.

Before me, on a small white plate, sat a bit of lamb, cut small and slim, just enough for two mouthfuls. It had been seared, spiced lightly with something fragrant that reminded me of springtime. A dainty row of puffy morels surrounded the slice of meat, with a spot of yellow gravy at its edge, a dollop of mint cream beneath this, one thin slice of boiled potato one layer down, a thick slice of crisp apple under, a spotting of maple syrup at its rim.

The conversation trickled. The music stopped. The sound of knives cutting took over.

We each took a bite. Small and perfect, the taste made me close my eyes. A feeling of pleasure went from tongue and upper palate down to the back of my throat, igniting a series of little shivers.

"Dear God." I opened my eyes, having forgotten that there were others at the table.

Stefan chuckled, nodding. "Good, isn't it?"

"Grand is what it is," Lucy said. "Holly's a magician with meats and sauces."

The sisters talked of summer days when they wandered among the vineyards, the sun itself seeming a companion, bog races, breath-holding contests, the May Pole in spring, winter rituals, amateur theatricals in Bright Colony, and tales of Auntie Rags as a girl. Stefan spoke of his new subjects at the women's prison and the orphanage two towns over and the explosion of art in Paris that took his breath away.

Enveloped in the deliciousness of food as course after course came out, I discovered an entire universe within the Windrow house.

Each course—duck, chopped fine, rolled with herbs and seductively smelly cheese into little hotcakes; spinach soufflé laid over truffles; the triangular cucumber toast with its horseradish mayonnaise; the lemoned butter melting into flaked cod atop a bed of ground pecans and pink clover blossom—small bites, just enough to create a sensation in the mouth, a sense of heaven.

Holly seemed a miracle worker—these chops and cuts, fish, fruits, quail, asparagus, ices, pâtés, hot and cold at the same time, all of it came out, one after the other, miniatures, little tastes, enough but not too much. Melted cocoa with a touch of hot chili freckled a thumb-sized scoop of vanilla ice cream atop a bed of thick lavender foam—heralding the end of it all.

A minute of silence followed. We each looked at our plates, at our glasses, at each other—stunned by magnificence.

Coffee arrived in demitasse cups, breaking the quiet.

Stefan stood and bowed to Holly when he came to collect the final plates. We clapped. We bravoed. Holly bowed to the table and offered up a brief speech about his mother's belief that a great dinner consisted of a thousand and one tastes. We laughed and told jokes that we knew. Sally leaned into me, and Lucy confessed that she'd hated me on sight but now had grown fond. An after-dinner drink tray magically appeared when we retired to the front parlor. Sally brought her cello out and Lucy sat at the piano. They began playing—masterfully—a beautiful lullaby, and then broke into a popular dance song of the day called "The Grizzly Bear." Holly squatted beside the piano, drawing a harmonica from his breast pocket, catching the tune.

I don't believe I had ever been so happy in all my life as that night, with the Cannibal Sisters and the artist who had given up his newspaper career and the son of the cook to Alejandra of Toledo and whose grandmother had been employed in the kitchen of the Empress—and whose father had hanged himself.

The transition from sleep to waking vanished.

Late in the morning, I opened my eyes. Sunlight came in from a nearby window.

The ceiling above was angled to a low pitched roof. The room was small. I glanced

to the right—my clothes had been laid out, as if laundered, on a chair by the bed.

My eyes closed, longing for sleep.

As I drifted up from half-sleep, I sensed that I was not alone in bed.

I turned to my left.

There, atop the heavy quilt, lay Catherine the Great in all her spotty glory.

The cheetah detected my wakefulness and began purring.

Holding my breath, I made my way with a series of small movements to the edge of the bed, clinging to the mattress with one hand, slipping to a crouching position on the floor.

The cheetah remained stretched out on its side, facing away from me. I rose up slowly and began dressing in hopeful silence. Drawing up my trousers, I reached for my shirt—never taking my eye off Catherine the Great.

I walked soft as a mouse across floorboards to the steep stair. It hit me, then: they had put me to bed in the attic room.

Taking a deep breath, I headed down the stairs barefoot, carrying my shoes.

I half-expected the wild cat to run after me, but I made it to the kitchen, where Lucy chatted with Holly as he scraped dishes from the previous night.

I offered to help with the cleanup, but Holly refused as a point of honor.

"Sleep well?" Lucy asked.

Holly—passing me a mug of coffee and a small plate of runny eggs—mentioned how they were afraid I was dead, I'd slept so long. He rattled off the news and rumors of the day, told to him by the man who brought the eggs that I had just begun eating as I stood there. The hurricane that everyone feared had headed out to sea far south of New England. A fisherman in Nova Scotia rescued a living baby from within the belly of a large codfish. (Lucy doubted this story, "but it's the news business, after all, and we know how that goes.") A car crashed in Bristol, many miles away, and everyone survived except a nun, who had only just taken her vow of chastity. Mrs. Trotter—of the village—ran off with the Miller boy who rode his horse right up to her front porch. Mr. Trotter was left to raise four children. There was more mingling of local gossip, genuine news and pulpy mythology until I'd finished my second cup, and felt no less sleepy.

I fumbled my way out to the back steps and sat down.

The sun headed toward noon in an un-clouded sky.

In the midst of yellow fields, Stefan stood painting at an easel. His subject seemed to be Sally, who crouched among low scrub.

As I approached them, I was shocked to see that she wore a scowl—and nothing else. Her clothes sat in a neat pile atop a long flat board several yards away.

She didn't look up at me when I walked by.

"She's pretending she's Catherine the Great, stalking the veldt for prey. Look." Stefan

brought me around to his work-in-prog-
ress, which was half-sketch, half paint. "The
Sphinx herself, I think. She's in character."

"In nude character," I said.

"We get a bit free here," he said. "If the
weather holds, you should stick around."

In the heat of day I took my shirt off and
sat down at the edge of the tall grass beside
Sally's clothes.

On top of the pile, the locket glinted in
the sun.

Pretending to nap, I lay down and reached
for the locket.

I fumbled with the hinge and latch until
the mechanism popped open. A thin per-
fume, conjuring violets and lilies, drifted up
from it.

A tiny faded photograph was pressed
within the locket. While I could tell it was a
man from the tie and collar, the area under

the forehead and above the collar was empty, the face rubbed out.

I closed the locket, and laid it back in its place. I thought of the mournful portrait of Sally beside the exuberant one of her sister, and the locket's role in bringing light into the dark painting.

Using my rolled-up shirt as a pillow, I stretched out on my back.

A hawk glided above me. Drowsy, I fell asleep again, the effects of the previous night's drinking still with me.

I sank into a dream of late night; I sat among a tree's thick branches, looking down at festivities below.

Sally and Lucy, much younger, danced with wild abandon around an enormous bonfire, accompanied by hysterics and mad-men all of whom sang strange hymns in a foreign language, with a melody both haunt-ing and painful to hear. As I took in this bi-zarre scene, I noticed the man who sat at the center of the fire, mouth open, screaming, yet unable to be heard above the increasing pitch of the insane chorus.

I recognized the man: it was myself. I noticed others sitting high in the branches of trees all around. Despite the shadows and leaf-cover, I made out the faces of men, all transfixed by the scene below. The woods were full of us—spectators to sacrifice.

I awoke to the hum of a bee and the whiteness of October sky.

Sally's face peered down from above. "We're done. Join me?"

Dressed in trousers and suspenders, she wore a white cotton shirt too large for her frame, a wide hat—not mine—on her head, her hair tucked up into it.

"It's exhausting to pose like that. Hours and hours. I ache all over." She informed me that Lucy and Stefan took off together in the infernal machine of a car and Holly bicycled to the village to replenish the kitchen "after

last night's massacre." She begged me to go for a walk down to the bog, and "maybe a swim. If you say no, I'll wheedle and whine."

"All right," I said, rising up, reaching for my shirt. My unsettling dream faded as reality etched itself all around.

"Like my outfit?" she asked as we walked by a garden, its vines heavy with flowers.

"Of course. It suits you."

"They're Holly's clothes. But fair's fair— he likes to wear mine sometimes. We trade around a bit."

The bohemian atmosphere appealed to me.

"I'm glad you're not leaving us," she said. And then suddenly, glancing across the garden. "Oh, look! A hummingbird. See? There?"

A blur of green and red dashed between the purple and blue flowers.

"Isn't it a beauty? You never see them this time of year. This is good luck. Make a wish, quick."

I closed my eyes and pretended to wish.

"What did you wish for?"

"Something private," I said, not wanting to lie to her if I could help it. "What about you?"

"I wished this moment would never end," she said. She looked among the branches and vines, expecting to see the bird again. "It always feels like my birthday when I spot a hummingbird. They're like fairies."

She led me down a path through shaded woods toward a clearing where the bog water glistened in dappled sunlight.

Sally slipped out of her clothes, a butterfly from its chrysalis, unaware that I ogled a bit without meaning to. She cautiously stepped into the water, twisting around to see if I would follow.

"Coming in?"

"A bog?" I asked. "That a good idea?"

"It's more pool than bog, you coward."

I hesitated, then to-helled-with-it, stripped down and splashed in beside her, shivering and laughing as I went.

I fought the natural feelings for her, this naked beauty—my cousin after all—seeing

her breasts, her hair down along her shoulders as if she were Eve herself—before the discovery of apple.

Afterward, we lay on the bank and stared up at the sky.

"Stefan tells me you're a reporter," she said.

"I should've been the one to tell you. Last night."

"I don't mind." She sat up and faced me.

I flopped, looking at her, the side of my face on a bed of moss.

She reached over and brushed hair back from my eyes. "We're not afraid of anything. Not the way you'd think. What'll you write?"

"Not sure yet."

"No one ever writes about Catherine the Great," she said. "You should make up a story about her. Maybe that she prowls the grounds and gobbles people up as if they were rabbits."

She sat up and reached toward her clothes. She picked up the locket and attached the chain behind her neck.

"What does it mean to you?" I asked.

"This?" She grasped the locket in her hand before letting it swing downward. She hesitated; her eyes narrowed. "My father gave it to me. My twelfth birthday. We both got one, but Lucy lost hers a long time ago. The very day that…well, the day things changed. I'm always afraid I'll lose it. So I wear it, every day. Every single day I remind myself." Then, she blushed, as if ashamed. "I feel as if…well, if I lost it, maybe something terrible will happen."

"Like an amulet. A charm."

"You understand," she said, her face lighting up. "I knew you would. It's a magic place, our home. It's protected."

I asked her the questions that I'd held back until then.

Later, dry and dressed, we returned to the house, all talked out.

Sally called for the cheetah, but the cat didn't return. She went to the living room to play Solitaire. I worried that I'd said some-thing wrong or made her feel uncomfortable.

I sat across from her, but we didn't speak for nearly an hour. Catherine the Great scratched at the back door.

When Sally went to let the cat in, I followed.

The cheetah had blood along its whiskers. "Ooh, good girl, good girl," Sally cooed. "She caught some wabbits."

Lucy strode in with Stefan at six. He looked beleaguered. He whined about some horrible woman in the village—one of the reporters who'd come to bother Lucy. They'd bought a gift for Sally—a little crystal bird all wrapped up in colored tissue. Holly put out a cold plate of vegetables and sliced ham on the kitchen table—a more subdued offering than the previous night's feast.

We picked at our plates, drank a bit, and the girls went off to flip through magazines, leaving Stefan with me on the porch as a brisk wind picked up. He smoked his pipe and we talked about things other than art and newspapers.

When we retired to the living room, the girls announced they were exhausted. "We wear out easily," Sally said as she kissed me on the forehead, while Lucy planted herself in Stefan's lap for a few seconds too long, arms around his neck. The Windrow sisters followed each other upstairs.

I sat up with Stefan listening to harp music on the Victrola.

He turned to me. "So, dig up some scandal to write about?"

"I'm not sure there is any. She told me about that week, though. What she could remember."

"And?"

"I'm not sure any of it happened. At least not the way it's been written up. I blame the father, I guess."

"Everybody did," he said. "What did she tell you?"

"That she and Lucy lived in a dollhouse in those days. That they got in trouble a lot. That they made up stories about people. They thought they were witches and made things happen. They thought ghosts wandered the woods all night long. She said the asylum patients were like uncles and aunts. Even Aunt Sapphronia was just another patient who did some light cleaning in the house. Nothing about murders or any of that."

After a minute, I added, "She told me it was as if she and Lucy lived inside a dream and they could never shake themselves awake. Until after. Long after."

"A dream," he said. "Well, no need to make sense of it. What happened, happened."

"I don't really understand how it could have happened. How two girls could have done it all."

"That's what confused the original investigation. There were too many possibilities," he said. "The suicide. The way Dr. Windrow was murdered. Conflicting testimonies. The girls themselves, physically unable to speak, believing they were under some curse."

"What do you make of it all?"

"I accept them," he said.

"But I still think about what they did. Are they the same two girls now that they were then?"

He answered my question with one of his own. "What's the worst thing you've ever done in your entire life—so far?"

I thought about it, ran through the various memories of bad things, sins of omission, lies, the people I might have unwittingly hurt in some way, the time I stole a magazine from the newsstand. "All right. Here goes."

I told him.

"How old were you?"

"Eleven. Maybe."

"Some people," he said, "do worse things. Some do less-worse. But are you the same boy now that you were then?"

"Of course not. But you can't compare the two. I hurt no one but myself. I got in trouble, but it was over when it was over. Lesson learned. Several people were killed here."

"But by whom?" he said. "Two girls, out of touch with the greater world around them? Mentally ill patients? A farmhand gone mad?"

I had no answer.

"We shed our skins," he said.

"What?"

"Like snakes, molting. We lose a skin and grow a new one. Many times over, during our lives."

I repeated my earlier question: "Are they the same two girls now that they were then?"

"I'm surprised you need to ask that."

"It's confusing."

"Of course. All those books and articles and Bog House of Horrors stories and the rhyme," he said. "Don't you see what's here? What they are? Who they are? Open your eyes."

"You've known them for years," I said. "Maybe that makes it easier."

"True. I first saw them at the Lyric Theater in Boston, long before I met them," he said. "They hadn't spoken since the night of the discoveries. The trauma had been too much. Their Uncle John did all the talking. He was a showman at that point. The lights, the audience, the little props he brought along. His tales of murder and blood, cannibalism and incest. They were like animals in a cage. I suspect they'd always been treated like that. And perhaps they did eat those bodies. Perhaps they did kill them. Or perhaps there's only slight truth in it.

"They've never really experienced the world. Oh, they buy things; they go to the village now and then. They read some magazines. They talk a good game. But they're untouched by the larger world. The most they've seen of it is that insane tour. But they don't know much beyond this stretch of land and sky. They've never read an actual newspaper. They read novels and serials. They get news as gossip, mostly. They don't know that they're much different from anyone else. They think most people go on lecture tours before the age of twenty. They think everyone grew up like this, under these circumstances. Their family home was an asylum."

He paused. "And it protects them. That legend. People are scared to come here much. When they do, Holly goes out and does his crazy act. Shoots a rifle or sets fire to weeds. That kind of thing. And they don't need the outside world anymore. They've never needed it. The bog and farm are enough for them. It's their magic circle."

Then, glancing upward, he said, "They've got the whole world here. Even the stars."

Following his gaze, I saw what I hadn't noticed before, when I'd entered the room the previous day, even though Sally turned down the lamps, just so I would see what was up above my head.

Stefan's words came to mind: *The light is always in the last place you'd think to look.*

The ceiling above had a vision of the heavens painted across it, a tiny but distinct glow to the stars and planets.

It was beautifully—startlingly—decan- descent.

A light in the darkness.

Early the next day, we went to pick mush-rooms in the woods for Holly's next dinner. When we found a rabbit in one of the traps, Lucy began sobbing like a child.

Sally grabbed her, whispering at her ear to calm her down. "They're watching us, even now," she said.

Stefan glanced over at me, as if this meant something.

I left at noon, with friendly kisses and hugs and promises to return. Sally's eyes filled with tears. I gave Catherine the Great a rub behind the ears.

Stefan drove me in Lucy's car all the way to the train station. He gave me a fatherly nudge on the shoulder before I got out of the car.

I stood on the train platform, imagining the story I would write about Bog House and the Cannibal Sisters; the bizarre dinner with its unusual meats and thick wine; the fear of sleeping in the spinster aunt's terrible room at the top of the attic stair—and the discovery of the dreaded map of the human body, exposing the choicest cuts from the human heart.